What Readers are Saying About *Just in Time*

"History can sometimes be long and tedious. The *Just in Time* books by Cheri Pray Earl and Carol Lynch Williams are short, believable tales that move along quickly with generous doses of suspense and action. Perfect for Common Core curriculums, students will find themselves quickly enveloped in page-turning narratives. A history treat for sure!"

—CARLA MORRIS, Provo City Library Children's Services Manager, member of American Library Association 2004 Caldecott Committee, author of *The Boy Who Was Raised by Librarians* (Peachtree Publications, 2007)

"A little something for everyone—history, humor, adventure, time travel . . ." —*Kirkus Reviews*

"I couldn't stop reading because I wanted to see if George and Gracie would get their mom and dad back."

—VAN, Age 6, Utah

• • •

"This story is like lemonade. Once you start, you can't stop. The story really draws you in, and you don't want to put it down until you're done. A definite 5-star rating!!!"

—BROCK, Age 12, Ohio

• • •

"*Just In Time* is a great series of fun, exciting stories and funny characters. I like when Gracie, George, and the others change into animals."

— BELLE, Age 8, Colorado

The Wizard of Menlo Park, New Jersey

To my tiny ones: Olivia and Jack,

Michael and Ben, and Charlotte.

—C.P.E.

For the Ellis Boys

—C.L.W.

Published by Familius LLC, www.familius.com

Familius books are available at special discounts for bulk purchases for
sales promotions, family or corporate use. Special editions, including
personalized covers, excerpts of existing books, or books with
corporate logos, can be created in large quantities for special needs. For
more information, contact Premium Sales at 559-876-2170 or email
specialmarkets@familius.com.

Library of Congress Catalog-in-Publication Data

2013957848

pISBN 978-1-938301-77-3
eISBN 978-1-939629-47-0

Printed in the United States of America

Edited by Amy Stewart
Cover and book design by David Miles

10 9 8 7 6 5 4 3 2 1

First Edition

JUST IN TIME

The Wizard of
Menlo Park, New Jersey

CHERI PRAY EARL AND
CAROL LYNCH WILLIAMS

ILLUSTRATIONS BY MANELLE OLIPHANT

MEET THE STOCKTON FAMILY

Matthew Stockton

Grandpa Stockton

Laura Stockton

Gracie   George

AND KEEP YOUR
EYES PEELED
FOR...

Crowe

Thomas
Edison

TRACK THE
ADVENTURE

 Delaware

 Pennsylvania

 New Jersey

It Happened Like This . . . I Swear

I'm George. And my sister's name is Gracie.

Gracie is nine years old. So am I.

We're twins. I'm older than she is by 5.75 minutes.

She's taller than me by one and a half inches.

But I'm smarter by about two feet.

Me and Gracie live with our grandpa. He's a fix-it man. He works at the Stockton Museum of Just About Everything in American History. Our family's museum.

Mom and Dad used to work here too.

Except we haven't really seen them for two years. Since they found the time machine.

That's when our trouble started.

Mom and Dad used the time machine to travel back in history. They bought great stuff for our museum. Then they got trapped in time. We never know where they are. Or where they will be. Or when.

We sure miss them. A lot.

Me and Gracie have a plan to get our parents back. We have to return all the stuff they bought for the Stockton Museum. Then Mom and Dad can come home.

The problem is, now we have to ride in the time machine.

And we have another big problem. Mr. Crowe.

He's stuck in time too. He's following us.

He wants us to take him to his time in 1879. In our time machine.

If we take him home before we return everything, before we rescue our parents . . . we might never see Mom or Dad again.

Then we might get trapped in time too.

CHAPTER 1

Off to See the Wizard

I reached toward the blinking red light on Grandpa's map of the United States.

Here's the thing.

That map is pinned to Grandpa's fix-it shop wall.

It's not plugged in anywhere.

So how's that light blinking?

How does it know where Mom and Dad are now?

That's what I wanted to find out.

"Don't mess with that, George," Grandpa said. He touched my shoulder. "You might get a shock. Or worse."

I had to know. I squinted and tapped the light with my finger.

Nothing happened.

"Whew," I said. "Nope. No shock. It's not even hot." I tried to sound like No Big Deal. But my legs wobbled. A lot.

"Who cares about that?" Gracie said. "Stop goofing around, George. Read where we're going next."

"Hold your horses . . . I mean, hold your horse, Gracie," I said. I laughed at my own joke. Because it was hilarious.

Grandpa covered a smile with his hand. "That never gets old," he said.

Gracie showed me her teeth. Like she did when she was a horse in Delaware. During the Revolutionary War. I backed away from her.

"Whatever, George," she said. She smiled a little too.

Grandpa read the map. He pointed to New Jersey. "Your mom and dad are in Menlo Park, New Jersey. In 1879," he said.

The time machine shook and shivered. "Bl-l-rrrr," it said.

I jumped.

So did Gracie. Right into me.

My glasses went all skewampus.

Grandpa didn't flinch. "I'll be," he said. He moved closer to the time machine.

The time machine looks like a regular old wardrobe now. But me and Gracie and Grandpa know better. In Delaware it looked like an outhouse. And in Pennsylvania, it was a car. It's a master of disguise.

Grandpa smoothed the doors with his hand. "Menlo Park, New Jersey," he said again.

The time machine shook harder than before. "Bl-l-rrrr," it said again.

That freaked me out because who knew it could make noises like that? I nudged my glasses up.

"Grandpa, don't," said Gracie. She held tight to her locket. The one Mom gave her.

I closed one eye. Menlo Park, New Jersey. Which is right where me and Gracie were going next.

To save our parents.

Grandpa didn't act like he heard Gracie. He walked to his desk and pulled out the big stack of papers. The papers tell us what Mom and Dad bought for the museum.

"I remember that," Grandpa said. He ran his finger down a page. "Yes, here it is. *Little Women*, by

Louisa May Alcott. Published in 1868."

"Huh?" me and Gracie said at the same time.

"Jinx," Gracie said. "Ha! You owe me a soda."

"Ding dang it," I said.

"You've heard of *Little Women*," Grandpa said. "The children's book?" He looked at us.

Gracie shook her head.

I didn't know either.

Grandpa scrunched his face all up. "Hmmm . . . I believe we have a copy in our Books from America exhibit."

He walked out of the fix-it shop.

We followed him into the dark museum. Past a Big Bird puppet in the Sesame Street exhibit. Around the statue of John Wayne sitting on a horse. Past the electric guitar exhibit. The exit signs glowed green above the doorways.

Grandpa walked fast. So did Gracie. I hurried to catch up.

Right in front of the Books from America exhibit, I ran into Gracie.

"Ow!" we both said at the same time.

I rubbed the front of my head. "Jinx," I said. "Ha! You owe *me* a soda."

Gracie rubbed the back of her head. "No. I don't," she said.

"Oh," I said. Her voice sounded like a boxing glove. One that wanted to punch me in the nose.

Grandpa switched on a light. Bookshelves and books covered this corner of the museum. From the floor to the ceiling. Grandpa ran his finger along a shelf. He pulled a brown book down. "I traveled back in time with your parents when they bought this," he said.

I stared at Grandpa. Then at Gracie. "You?" I said.

"Yes," said Grandpa. "New Jersey is a great place. I met Thomas Edison there."

"The guy who invented electricity?" Gracie asked.

"Uh, Gracie," I said. I swallowed a super gigantic laugh. "Thomas Edison didn't invent electricity. He invented the light bulb." I tapped the side of my head. "Brains of the family, remember?"

Gracie frowned. "Whatever, George."

"Mr. Edison was a genius," Grandpa said. He looked sort of dreamy. Like he wished he could meet Mr. Edison again. "The newspaper reporters at the time called him the Wizard of Menlo Park."

Grandpa opened the book. "See this?" he said and held it out to us.

I peered at the name "Thomas A. Edison" written in cursive on the first page. "Cool," I said.

"Wow," Gracie said. "How did you get that?" She traced the signature with her finger.

"I ran into Mr. Edison in a store near Menlo Park," said Grandpa. "Your mom and dad wanted to buy a book for the museum. That's when Mr. Edison walked in." Grandpa smiled. "I asked him to sign our book. We had a nice talk."

Grandpa is sort of a scientist too. He can figure out how to fix anything in the museum. Maybe that's why he likes Thomas Edison so much.

We walked back to the fix-it shop. I watched the wardrobe as we walked past. It didn't move. It didn't make a sound.

I glanced at the clock by the map. It was after midnight. Way past bedtime. But me and Gracie couldn't go to bed yet. We had to take another trip. To New Jersey. Mom and Dad needed us to go. And if we were lucky, me and Gracie might see more than just a glimpse of them this time.

"You kids need to get some sleep," Grandpa said.

"I'm not tired," Gracie said.

"Me either," I said. Sometimes me and Gracie stay in the past for days. Then we come home in the time machine. But our clock says we've only been gone for a few seconds.

"I never got tired when I time traveled, either," said Grandpa. "No matter how long I was gone. Like time stood still."

He closed *Little Women* and put it in my hands. "Tell Mr. Edison hello for me," Grandpa said.

I hate this part. The part where me and Gracie leave.

Grandpa worries about us traveling in time. But he can't go. He might get stuck in time too. Like our parents. Then what would happen to me and Gracie?

Gracie took his hand. "We'll be okay, Grandpa," she said. "We have to go. Mom and Dad can't ever get home if we don't."

Grandpa nodded. "I love you kids," he said.

"I know," me and Gracie said together.

"Jinx," said Grandpa. "You both owe me a soda pop. When you get back from Menlo Park—oops!" he said.

The time machine shook again. Hard.

"Uh-oh," I said. My stomach did a somersault.

The time machine shivered.

"Oh, no," Gracie said. She held her locket.

The wardrobe doors flew open. A heavy wind pulled on me and Gracie and Grandpa.

Gracie stumbled forward. So did I.

"Grandpa!" I yelled over the wind.

Papers swirled around the room. A chair tipped over. A glass fell off the worktable and broke.

Grandpa caught hold of his desk. He grabbed onto my shirt. "Take Gracie's hand, George," he said. His voice was loud.

Gracie slid toward the time machine.

I dropped the book and reached for her.

Little Women flew past us and inside the wardrobe.

Me and Gracie locked hands.

The wardrobe doors slammed shut.

The wind stopped.

I screamed like a girl.

Gracie raised her eyebrows. "You screamed," she said, "like a girl."

"I got freaked out," I said. What else could I say? My whole body jiggled like Jell-O.

"What's wrong with the time machine?" Gracie asked. She still held my hand. "It never just takes us. Not until we're ready to go, anyway."

Grandpa shook his head. "I don't know. I think

it's nervous to go"—he lowered his voice—"to you-know-where."

Gracie dropped my hand. She walked to the time machine.

I tiptoed behind her.

She pulled on the doors. They wouldn't open.

"What's wrong?" Gracie said.

"I'm scared, that's what," I whispered.

"Not you, George," said Gracie. "I'm talking to the time machine."

"Oh," I said.

Grandpa walked next to Gracie.

He put his hand on the doors. "They have to go," he said. "And I'm counting on you to take care of them."

The wardrobe trembled. I felt tremble-y too.

"We'll be okay," Gracie said in a quiet voice. "Whatever happens. Me and George have each other"—she petted the doors—"and we have you. So please. Open up so we can go and save our parents."

Grandpa smiled at Gracie. "Good girl," he said.

The doors cracked open.

"Yikes," I said. I hugged Gracie's arm.

"It's all right, George," Grandpa said. "Don't be afraid. You can both get in now."

Gracie climbed inside the wardrobe and sat

down. Cross-legged. She picked up *Little Women*. "Are you coming, George?" she said. "We have a job to do."

That's my sister. Brave, bossy Gracie.

I nodded and climbed up next to her. Even though my legs shook like crazy.

Grandpa touched our faces. "Whatever is worrying the time machine is waiting for you in Menlo Park. So watch out."

The time machine quivered.

I nodded. Gracie did too.

The time machine made a whirring sound. It lit up.

"Crowe will be there like always," Grandpa said. "Waiting for his chance to grab you and the time machine." He kissed my forehead and then Gracie's. "Stay together."

The whirring sound got louder and louder. Lights flashed.

Grandpa stepped back.

We waved to him.

"Here we go, Gracie," I said.

She held my hand.

Then BANG! the doors slammed shut.

And ZOOM! we were inside a black hole.

CHAPTER 2

Bird Brain

The time machine landed with a thump. Newspapers swirled all around us.

"Look, George," I said. I stretched my arms out long. Then I stretched out my neck.

Whew. I could see everything. No dark barn like in Pennsylvania. "It's daylight."

We were between two buildings. In an alley. A dirty alley. It stunk like garbage.

But there was plenty of light and air. Cold air that blew at me.

I shivered.

"This is going to be easy peasy," I said. "Let's

get this over with, George. I want to hurry and get Mom and Dad back."

Happiness filled me up. Every adventure, we were that much closer to Mom and Dad.

"Right, Gracie," George said. He looked at me. His eyes grew huge.

"Has the time machine turned into a cage?" I said. Sure looked like it. I was perched on a little wooden swing. "Get the door open, George. Quit staring at me."

"Okay." George fumbled with the latch. Like he couldn't wait to get out of there. He crawled out, leaving the little door open behind him.

"It's a birdcage, huh?" I said. "A nice one too." The bars were thin pieces of wood. Polished. Shiny. "You're not wearing tights, George. Good thing, right?"

A page of newspaper lay on the floor below me. I tipped my head to the side so I could see better. The paper had the words THOMAS ALVA EDISON printed on it.

Grandpa's favorite guy!

Was he doing something important? Or was he always in the newspaper? Was Mr. Edison famous? A cold puff of wind blew the paper up against the bars.

I tipped my head and looked the other way. A city bustled a few steps beyond us.

"Here's how it goes," I said. I peered at George through the bars. "We take the book to the store. You think they got a Barnes and Noble here? Then we climb back in this cage and go home."

George cleared his throat. He leaned down. Put his face close to mine. "You should take a deep breath, Gracie." He seemed huge. Bigger than when he was in the cage with me.

Two men walked past on the street at the end of the alley. One wore a tall hat. They didn't even look at us.

"Plus," I said, "we keep a look out for Crowe. You know how he is. Sneaky."

I grinned at George.

George took a step back. "Don't make that face, Gracie. It scares me," he said.

"I was thinking," I said. I lifted my foot up to scratch my head. Right behind my ear. "This thing is small enough for us to keep it close by. We can carry the time machine around and everything. That way Crowe will never get it."

"Speaking of crows," George said.

He squeezed his eyes shut.

He shook his head.

He rubbed at his nose.

"Take a look in the mirror, Gracie. The one with the bell on it. Do it slow and careful."

Now wait a minute. It's my job to be bossy. I tried to raise an eyebrow. My face felt stiff. My necklace clinked against the time machine.

"Why?" I squinted at George. Sort of.

Then I eased my way sideways across the swinging bar. Clenching it with my toes.

It sure was cold. The newspaper fluttered.

"Just do it," George said.

"Okay," I said. "After that we gotta get indoors. I shouldn't be out in this weather. Is it snowing?"

I tried to see the sky. Way up there were the building tops. They were so high, they seemed to lean toward each other. Then way way WAY up there was the sky. Gray as a dove.

Slow, fat flakes floated down onto me and George.

George lifted the cage till we were looking right at each other.

"You sure look pretty, Gracie," he said. "Prettier than normal."

I eyed him.

"And you have pants to your ankles this time, George," I said. "Is that a velvet jacket you're wearing?"

Then . . . Wait. A. Minute.

Since when did George care what I looked like?

When I changed from human to . . .

Quick as I could I made my way to the mirror. I stuck my arms out to keep my balance. A feather floated to the cage floor.

"What?"

I squawked.

I mean I let out a real, live, bird-like squawk.

Not me!

Not again!

It should always be George who changes into something else. Into a rat. Or into . . .

I already knew the answer.

I looked in the mirror.

A parrot face stared back at me.

Orange bill.

Creamy white chest.

Lime green wings with teal blue under feathers.

Another cold wind blew down the alley. It brushed through my feather tips.

"Maybe I should lock you up in there, Gracie,"

George said. He spun the cage a little by the handle he held. "You look kind of . . . ruffled." He laughed.

"Stop that, George," I said. "You're making me dizzy. This is cruelty to animals. You want to see some parrot puke?"

I let out a sigh.

Not fair.

A parrot.

Me. A parrot in Menlo Park in 1879.

"What I want to know is how did *you* fit in the cage?" I said. I put my wings on my hips. I think they are hips. "How did you get so big all of a sudden?"

George shrugged. "Magic, I guess. Like everything else we do nowadays."

I let out a longer sigh.

"I guess," I said. "It's still weird, George."

George wrapped his arms around the cage. "Let's get going," he said.

"That's what I've been telling you all along," I said.

George stepped out of the alley onto the brick sidewalk. A row of shops were across the street. And on both sides of us.

"First get me out of here, George. You can see I don't have thumbs."

George stopped long enough to reach in the cage. I gave him a nip.

"Hey!" George said. He pulled his hand out and sucked on his finger.

"Don't keep Gracie in a cage," I said. "I let you ride on my shoulder when you were a rat. Remember that icky tail? But take a look at me. I am beautiful." I fluttered onto my brother's hand.

I puffed up my chest.

Walked up his arm to his shoulder.

And as I did, Crowe walked right past us. Close enough to touch.

He didn't seem to even notice me and George.

"He's found us already," George said. There was fear in his voice.

My head bobbed like a bathtub toy. I couldn't make it stop. "Run, George," I said. But it came out like "Awk! Awk!"

Crowe just kept going.

George turned the opposite way of Crowe. Almost running.

The time machine swinging like a pendulum.

We had to get rid of this book and go home.

Now.

CHAPTER 3

As the Crowe Flies

"Ow! Gracie, your claws are digging into my skin."

I tried to shoo her off my shoulder with my head. But she didn't shoo. "Why can't you ride in the cage?"

"I get cage sick. I get cage sick," Gracie said. She ruffled her feathers.

"I heard you the first time," I said.

My feet slid along the icy sidewalk. The birdcage banged against my shins. Ding dang it!

This place was colder than a frozen pickle.

I looked in every store window. No bookstore. "Where's the Barnes and Noble?" I said. I held *Little Women* inside my jacket. Away from the snowflakes falling down on us.

"Awk!" Gracie said in her sandpaper voice. "Hurry up, George. Hurry up. It's freezing out here. It's freezing out here. And Crowe. Crowe!"

My teeth chattered like a monkey. "I am hurrying," I said. "What's with the double-talk?"

"I don't know, I don't know," Gracie said. "Darn it. Awk! Darn it."

We passed a horse and buggy parked on the muddy street. The horse whinnied to Gracie.

"Right back at you," she said. "Right back at you."

That's when it happened. In front of the bakery window.

I slipped on an icy patch. My feet went flying out in front of me.

Gracie squawked. She dug her claws deeper into me. Man did that hurt.

I screamed and grabbed at her.

The birdcage hit the ground with a BANG!

So did I.

Gracie flew off my shoulder. She landed on top of the cage.

Little Women went PLOP! into a slushy puddle of water.

My heart went PLOP! too.

"Uh, oh. Uh, oh," Gracie said. "That's bad. That's bad. Awk!"

I pulled *Little Women* out of the puddle. Water dripped off the cover.

I stood up. My shoulder hurt. Like somebody had stabbed me with a knife.

"This time travel stuff is for the birds," I said. I wished I could laugh. "Get it Gracie? For the birds?"

Gracie didn't laugh. "What do we do, George? What do we do?" she said. "The book is ruined. The book is ruined."

She held her locket chain in her beak. Her eyes went wide.

"First off," I said, "don't freak out on me." I brushed the snow off my pants. "Second of all, stop saying everything two times."

Gracie opened her orange beak. No words came out. Not even an Awk!

Nothing.

Nothing.

Now I was worried. I held my hand out to her. She hopped up on it. I put my face close to hers. "Gracie?" I said. I tapped her green head.

"I'm doing deep breathing," she said. "Deep

breathing. Awk!"

"Can parrots do that?" I said, because I didn't think they could.

Gracie stared at me. The silver locket dangled from her beak. She didn't say anything.

Nothing.

Nothing.

"It calms me down," she said.

"Hey, Gracie," I said. "You only said that once."

Gracie smiled. Sort of. Like a parrot does.

The locket chain fell out of her beak. "I'm okay now, George," she said.

"That's good, Gracie," I said. I showed her the book.

"We're supposed to return everything the way it was." Gracie took another deep breath. "Not ruined. Now Mom and Dad will be stuck forever."

"Don't worry," I said. Even though I was worried. Sick-to-my-stomach worried. "I'll think of something."

The door to the bakery flew open. A little girl wearing a long coat and black boots ran out. A man followed after her. "Dot," he said in a voice like a fire alarm.

Dot pushed her brown hair back from her face.

"Hi," she said. She sniffed and wiped her nose on her ruffled sleeve. She stared straight at Gracie. "Can I hold your bird?"

"That would be fun," I said. I smiled as big as I could at Gracie.

She didn't laugh again. "Awk!" she said. "No touchy." She hopped farther up my shoulder.

"What a beautiful bird," the man said. "A Quaker parrot?"

I nodded like I knew.

"What's its name?" he asked. He offered Gracie a cookie from his pocket.

She took it in her beak and chomped it. Crumbs fell on the front of my jacket.

"Gracie," I said. "I'm George."

"What did you say?" the man asked. He leaned toward me. "I don't hear well."

"Gracie," I said louder. "And George."

The man smiled. "Nice to meet you. My name is Tom."

Dot stepped closer.

"Gracie doesn't like to be touched," I said.

Dot and Gracie were nose to nose.

"Danger," Gracie squawked.

Dot reached up with one chubby hand.

I felt Gracie lean back and back and back.

"Umh . . ." I said.

"No, Dot," Tom said. He pulled her away.

"But Daddy," Dot said. "I want to pet it."

Tom patted Dot's hand. "Let's not forgot the poor parakeet you petted yesterday."

Gracie wobbled on my shoulder like she might faint. "Poor parakeet?" she said.

"Nice to meet you, George and Gracie," Tom said. "Maybe we'll see you both tonight. At the New Year's Eve light show. In Menlo Park."

He tipped his hat. Dot held his hand as they walked down the sidewalk. She kept turning back to look at us.

"Menlo Park?" I said. I looked at Gracie.

"Aren't we in Menlo Park, George?" she said.

I turned to ask Tom. I didn't see him or Dot anywhere. Not on the sidewalk. Not in the street. Not back in the bakery. "That's weird," I said. How did they do that?

"Look over there, George," Gracie said. "I think we're in Metuchen."

"Did you see Tom and Dot disappear?" I said. I watched to see if they would come out of a store. Or maybe they would ride by in their buggy.

Gracie pecked my cheek. "Pay attention, George."

"Ouch—okay, okay," I said. I rubbed my face. "What's Metuchen?"

"This town," she said. "See that store across the street?" She pointed her wing. "*Metuchen Dry Goods* is painted on the front."

A man rode a horse down the street. Dirty snow was everywhere.

"Great," I said. "So the time machine dumped us in the wrong town. In the middle of winter." I covered my ears with my hands to warm them up. "Let's ask somebody where Menlo Park is. Before we turn into ice statues."

"Good idea," Gracie said. "But watch out for Crowe. He could be anywhere. Waiting for us."

The snow stopped falling but the air was still freezing. The sun peeked out of the clouds for a second.

Gracie hopped up on my shoulder. I grabbed the birdcage. I tucked *Little Women* inside my jacket. The book felt soggy.

We headed down the sidewalk.

A woman walked toward us. Her long blue dress swept the ground. She winked at me. "Pretty bird," she said.

"Thank you," said Gracie.

The woman stopped. "What a sweet thing," she said. She petted Gracie's head.

"Excuse me, ma'am. Do you know where Menlo Park is?" I said.

"About two miles that way." She pointed. "Follow the Lincoln Highway."

She smiled and walked on.

"Did you see that?" Gracie said. "I talked to that lady. And she didn't get all weird. I think she likes me."

An idea popped into my head. "I have a plan, Gracie," I said.

"Awk!" Gracie said. "We're in trouble now."

"No, it'll be okay," I said. "You can give the book away to Mr. Edison. He'll take it from you because he loves birds. I watched a show about him. On National Geographic."

"I don't know, George," Gracie said. "What if it doesn't work? What if he doesn't want a ruined book? What happens to us?"

"What if it does? What if Mom and Dad show up when we give the book to Mr. Edison?" I said. "We have to try at least."

Gracie pecked me on the ear.

"Ouch," I said. "What was that for?"

"There's Crowe, George," she said. Sort of whispery. Sort of scared.

A horse and buggy blocked my view. When it passed, I saw Crowe. Standing on the sidewalk. Straight across the street from us.

"Oh, no," I said. My stomach fell like a stone in a swimming pool.

Crowe looked right at us.

"Awk!" Gracie said. "Hide in the barbershop, George." She pointed with her wing.

In two giant steps I was through the door. Me and Gracie peeked out the front window.

Crowe crossed the street. Like he didn't know us.

"What's going on?" Gracie said.

"I don't know," I said. My heart thumped. But it was warm here in the barbershop.

"It's a trick," Gracie said. She stretched out her wings. "He's setting a trap for us. We've got to get to Mr. Edison's house."

"Hair cut, young man?" the barber said. He was so bald his head was shiny.

"No thanks," I said and dashed out the door. The birdcage clanked against my leg. Gracie pulled at my jacket.

We headed in the direction of Mr. Edison's laboratory.

"Two miles is a long way to walk, George," Gracie said. "Let's get a ride."

"From who?" I said. "Too bad you're not a horse this time too."

"Too bad you're not a horse this time too," Gracie said.

"Stop it," I said.

"Stop it," she said. She squawked. Which is like laughing for a parrot. I think.

"You're not funny," I said.

"You're not funny," she said.

We walked out of town on the Lincoln Highway. Like the lady told us to. A horse and buggy passed us. Then another one. We walked until my legs hurt. Until my face and hands felt numb from the cold. Plus my arms were tired of carrying Gracie's cage. And my side was wet from carrying the book.

I stopped to rest. "I wish I had my scooter," I said.

"Stick your thumb out, George," Gracie said.

"I'm not doing that," I said. "It's embarrassing. Besides. Who knows what that means in 1879."

We kept going. After a while my feet were ice blocks.

Gracie snuggled up next to my ear. She shivered. "I'm cold, George," she said. "Stick your thumb out. Just try it."

So I did. To show her it wouldn't work.

A buggy stopped beside us.

"I can't believe it," I said.

"I can't believe it," Gracie said.

"Not now, Gracie," I said.

"Need a ride?" a man's voice called out from inside the buggy.

I couldn't see him.

"Told you so," said Gracie.

I ignored her.

"Thanks, Mister," I said. "Thanks a lot."

"Don't mention it," the man said. He leaned forward.

And I looked right into Crowe's smiling face.

CHAPTER 4

Being a Bird Is All Cracked Up

"Gracie, stop, please," George said.

I gripped George's shoulder with my claws. I tried to relax, but Crowe was grinning right in my face. Who can relax when your sworn enemy is looking you in the eyeball?

Wind gusted down the highway, like it wanted to push us back toward town.

I was ready to go.

All the way back.

George stood halfway in, halfway out of the buggy. He held onto the time machine birdcage. His shoes were wet from the snow.

His hair stuck up this way and that.

My feathers would probably break right off. Even though the sun was sort of out, it didn't feel warm.

"Shouldn't you get us out of here?" That's what I wanted to whisper in George's ear. Seeing as I was perched right there by it. I leaned close to him. Then I squawked out, "Run! Run!"

"Thank you, Mister," George said. He turned from the carriage. "My bird is health conscious. She wants us to run."

"Good one, George," I said. "Good one."

I meant it.

Crowe smiled again. He let out a happy laugh. "You know who would love you?" He was closer now. He poked right at my feathered belly that I must admit is beautiful.

I snapped at him but missed Crowe's gloved finger.

"Why I oughtta . . ." I said.

"The Wizard," Crowe said.

George cleared his throat.

"That's real nice," George said. "Me and Gracie, we got to get back home. We can't see wizards or anything."

"There's a party planned for tonight," Crowe said. "To celebrate New Year's Eve. I shouldn't have left but I had to run an errand. I have to get this medicine to my little Scarlett."

Squeeze.

"Stop it, Gracie," George said. "We'll go this way." George sort of pointed.

Crowe said, "I can give you a hand. We have to hurry. There's so much to get ready for the celebration. Jump on in."

I checked behind us.

Wait. A. Minute.

I could turn my head all the way back. And all the way to the front. Back. Front. Wow! This trick might come in handy.

"Ditch," I said. "Watch the ditch."

George stopped walking backwards. Good thing too or else he would have fallen.

Again.

And I would have had to fly away.

Laughing.

Then George would be at the mercy of Crowe. All by himself.

"We'll stop at my house," Crowe said. "Afterwards I'll run you over to Tom. He'd love to meet you."

Crowe stretched across the seat, the reins in his hands. He pointed at my belly.

"Don't think so," I said. I didn't even have to work at the squawky sound. It happened on its own.

The horse pulling Crowe's buggy looked over at me.

I nodded at it.

The horse nodded back.

"Who's Scarlett?" George said. He walked forward again. "Who's Tom?"

"Scarlett's my little girl," Crowe said. "Tom is the Wizard. Don't tell me you've never heard of Tom Edison?" Crowe stared at George. "He's the most famous inventor in the world. I work with him and his other muckers. We're his assistants. In Tom's Invention Factory in Menlo Park."

"Menlo Park?" George said. He looked at me. I looked at him.

"Menlo Park?" I said.

Crowe laughed. "That's quite a bird you have there."

"You don't even know," George said. "We know about Thomas Edison. He says 'ninety-nine percent perspiration—'"

Squeeze.

"I mean . . ." George gave me a long side-eyed look.

I tipped my head at him. Just like a bird would. One side. The other. One side. The other. Now I knew why all birds did that. So they could give someone a good, hard stare with both eyes.

"I mean, I have something to give Mr. Edison," George said.

"Danger. Danger, Will Robinson," I said.

Crowe gave me a funny look.

George pushed at me. "I gotta talk to the bird a second."

"I can wait only a moment," Crowe said. "My wife will wonder if I've gotten lost in time."

"I bet," I said. Sort of whispering.

George moved close to the horse.

The horse showed its teeth.

"Good day," I said.

"Listen, Gracie," George said. "I'm eating you for dinner if you pinch me again. It hurts. And something is weird here. That"—George pointed back at Crowe, who smiled and waved—"is not the Crowe we know. He's like a different person."

"Why do you say that?" I said.

"Are you a bird brain?" George shook his head.

"Think about it. This Crowe smiles a lot. He has a daughter named Scarlett. He isn't trying to steal our time machine. Besides, he works with Thomas Edison. He happens to be on his way to where we need to go. And I don't want to walk."

I nodded. Once I got my head going it was hard to stop.

"You're right," I said.

Another buggy came up from town. Yup! I had great eyesight as a bird.

"I can fly," I said to George. Just so he would know.

He ignored me. "We've landed in Crowe's time. When he's younger. And still nice."

I flapped my arms a little. My arms disguised as wings.

"This young Crowe," George said, "has a family. He works with an inventor. Grandpa's favorite inventor, Gracie."

Flap flap flap. Nod nod nod.

George walked up to Crowe. "You know what, Mister Crowe?" George said. "My sister the bird . . . I mean, my sister's bird, and I would love to catch a ride with you."

"Excellent," Crowe said. "Climb aboard. This is

one of our coldest winters ever. You'd never make it all the way without freezing to death. It's a good thing I stopped."

"Thank you," George said.

George climbed up on the seat. He settled the birdcage time machine between his knees.

"Here. Tuck this around you." Crowe lifted a blanket for George.

I snuggled in with him. Pretty soon only my eyes showed.

"Let's go," Crowe said. He flicked the reins and we started off down the road.

"It's early for you two to be out," Crowe said.

George nodded. "Our grandfather sent us on an errand."

Almost true.

"We have to return a book."

We were pretty far out of town now. There were fewer and fewer houses out this way.

"Which book is that?" Crowe said.

George took out the damp *Little Women*. "I dropped it," he said.

Crowe nodded. "I see that," he said. "Did you like it?"

"I heard the movie was better," George said.

"Excuse me?" Crowe said.

"Err," George said.

"No more talking," I said. "No more talking, George."

"I've been reading *20,000 Leagues Under the Sea*," Crowe said. "So many adventures."

He smiled.

"I love the thought of inventing a machine that lets you go to the bottom of the ocean," Crowe said.

I pecked at George so he would stay silent. No need to talk about submarines right now.

"That's the wonderful thing about working with Thomas Edison." Crowe adjusted the blanket. "If I have an idea, I talk to him. We work on my inventions too. But . . ."

"But what?" George said.

The fast-moving buggy was closer.

"If I had Edison's money, well"—Crowe stared at the road ahead—"I could find a cure for my little girl's cough. I could have the patents all to myself. Make a name for my family and me. I wouldn't have to share anything."

Crowe looked at me and George.

"There can be two wizards at Menlo Park, don't you think?" Crowe said. His face got all worried.

"One wizard, me, could invent something that saves people who are sick."

"Like Scarlett?" George said.

"Yes," Crowe said. "Like Scarlett."

He said it so sad my little birdy eyes got all wet. From the cold, of course. Not tears.

Now the other buggy passed us.

A passenger peeked out. He tipped his hat. Winked.

Another Crowe. The old, bad Crowe.

What's he doing here? I squawked so loud this time George covered his ears.

"Ouch," George said.

I guess I don't have to sit on his shoulder for him to complain.

"Gracie," George said. "I'm going to pluck you bald if you scream again."

"Crowe," I said. "Crowe."

I hopped up and down on the seat. Sort of. The blanket fell off my shoulders and around my black feet. Just like that, I was cold.

Old Crowe in the buggy ahead of us disappeared from view.

Young Crowe laughed. "That little Quaker parrot of yours is something else," he said. "It sounded like she said my name."

"Two of them," I said to George, whispering. It's not easy to whisper when you are a parrot. Trust me. "Two."

How could this be?

A nice young Crowe here.

A terrible, time-machine-stealing older Crowe riding off down the road. Headed in the direction we were.

Right toward Menlo Park.

Right toward the New Year's Eve celebration.

Right toward Thomas Edison.

Like he had done this all before.

CHAPTER 5

Connect the Dots

We stopped in front of a small house. Smoke twisted up from the chimney.

Young Crowe jumped from the buggy. He pulled a package from his pocket. "I'll be only a minute," he said. He walked into the house.

The horse stamped his foot and whinnied. The buggy shook.

"Do you think Scarlett dies in the future, Gracie?" I said. I pulled the blanket to my chin.

"Why did you say that, George?" She pecked at my hair.

"Because Old Crowe is a bad guy. But he wasn't

always. What else would make him so mean?" I said.

"I don't know," Gracie said. She cocked her head sideways. "That would be sad if Scarlett died. I wonder what's wrong with her."

"You know what?" I said. "We could take Scarlett to our time. In the time machine. Our doctor could fix her I bet."

"That would never work, George," Gracie said. "What if she got stuck with us forever? She'd never see her family again, that's what."

I swallowed.

"Like you and me might never see Mom and Dad again," I said.

It was an awful thought.

Crowe walked out of the house. He called through the open door. "I'll check on you later," he said. "I love you all." He pulled the door closed.

His face was tight. He clenched his jaw.

Crowe climbed in the buggy. He covered his legs with the blanket. "Hee-yah," he said and snapped the reins.

The horse trotted down the road.

I wanted to help. But I didn't know what to do. I said, "I'm sorry about your daughter."

I don't think Crowe heard me. He didn't say a

word. He stared straight ahead.

"He must be worried about Scarlett," I whispered to Gracie.

She blinked at me. Nodded.

Clouds covered the sun again. Snowflakes fell into the buggy. Gracie hid in her part of the blanket. I hid in mine.

Crowe was quiet the rest of the trip.

Soon we got to Mr. Edison's laboratory. Crowe stopped the buggy in front.

"Book, George," Gracie said. She peeked at me over the cover. With one eye. "Birdcage."

"I've got it," I said. I patted *Little Women*.

Men worked outside stringing lights and putting up decorations.

"What's everyone doing?" I asked.

"That's for the party tonight," said Crowe. "Thomas has the bulbs hung on all the buildings. Then all the way down Christie Street. Imagine what this place will look like when the lights go on. He wants to show the people his new long-burning electric bulb."

Crowe spoke soft.

My stomach went PLUNK! because I was here. At the genius inventor's laboratory.

And on a party night too.

Gracie ruffled her feathers. She climbed up Crowe's arm. She turned around and around on his shoulder. "Off to see the Wizard," she said.

"That's catchy, Gracie," Crowe said. "Off to see the Wizard."

I jumped out of the buggy. "Wow," I said. There were workers everywhere.

"Run on inside, George," Crowe said.

"Cool!" I said. "Thanks."

Crowe scrunched his eyebrows together. "It *is* cool today," he said. "You're welcome."

I ran up the steps. Through the front doors of the laboratory. Ta dah! I was inside Thomas Edison's laboratory.

"What's burning?" I said.

"Everything," Crowe said. He walked up beside me. Gracie perched on his shoulder.

"Mr. Edison burns all kinds of materials for his experiments."

The whole room was lit with lamps. Lamps on cabinets. On shelves. Hanging from the ceiling.

Men wearing lab coats ran from table to table. Like they were in a big fat hurry. Shelves crammed with bottles stood against the walls.

An organ sat at the back of the room.

"Why do you have an organ in an inventor's shop?" I asked.

"Sometimes after work, Tom plays and we sing," Crowe said. "We work long hours in the Invention Factory. That's how we relax."

"Invention Factory," I said. I was too excited to stand still. So I hopped around. "Grandpa would love this place. It's fun."

Gracie bobbed up and down. "Grandpa would love this place," she said.

Crowe laughed. "What a smart bird you are, Gracie," he said. "I can't wait for Thomas to see you."

"Smart bird," she said. She grinned a parrot grin.

"Where *is* Mr. Edison?" I said.

"Thomas," Crowe said in a loud voice. "Can you spare a moment?"

A man looked up from a table. He had dark hair. He wore goggles. It was Mr. Edison. A lot younger than the photo I saw on National Geographic.

My stomach squiggled and squiggled. The man from the candy shop.

"Mr. Edison doesn't hear well," said Crowe. "You'll have to speak up when you talk to him."

"I know," I said.

Mr. Edison walked toward us. Dot ran out from behind him. "Can I hold the bird now, Father?" she said.

"Awk!" Gracie said. She flew up and landed on a cabinet.

"Thomas," Crowe said in a loud voice. "I'd like you to meet George and his pet bird, Gracie. George, this is the Wizard of Menlo Park."

Mr. Edison lifted his goggles. He smiled. "George. I didn't expect to see you and Gracie so soon." Mr. Edison pulled a cookie out of his pocket. He offered it to Gracie. "Will you come down for a snack, Gracie?" he said.

"I see you've met," said Crowe.

"Here birdy birdy birdy," said Dot. She whistled. She clapped her hands. "Here, Gracie."

Gracie walked on the edge of the cabinet. "No touchy," she said. She didn't come down.

I looked around the room. "This place is like a carnival. For inventors," I said.

Mr. Edison cupped his hand over one ear. "What was that, George?"

"It's like a carnival." I yelled this time.

Mr. Edison smiled. "We do have fun here," he said.

"Fun, Thomas?" Crowe said in a loud voice. "We work hard. We make history here."

Crowe spoke to me. "Why, we invented the electric light bulb in this room. Just a couple of weeks ago."

Mr. Edison frowned. "Now, Charles. Don't exaggerate. We didn't invent the light bulb. We figured out how to make the filament burn longer. Which is better than anyone else has been able to do, I'll grant you that."

"You sure are a genius, Mr. Edison," I said.

Dot scooted a chair next to the cabinet.

"Danger, George," said Gracie. Her neck feathers stuck straight up.

I didn't blame her.

"Thomas didn't create his inventions alone, George," said Crowe. His voice was quiet now. He sounded bothered. "Everyone in this room helped. Truth be told, I helped the most."

"What's that you said, Charles?" Mr. Edison said. He leaned toward me and Crowe. "Blast it. I can't hear a thing with all the noise in here."

"Nothing, Thomas," Crowe said.

Dot climbed up on the chair. She reached for Gracie. "Come down, birdy," she said.

Gracie stepped away from Dot.

"No, Dot," said Mr. Edison. He pulled her off the chair. "Leave that beautiful creature alone."

Mr. Edison turned to Crowe.

"Now, Charles," Mr. Edison said. "Let's talk about that little girl of yours. How is she?"

Crowe shook his head. "We're worried, but expecting a miracle."

"What's wrong with her?" I asked.

"It's her lungs," Crowe said. He ran his hand over his eyes.

"Medicine," Gracie said from above.

"Right, Gracie," I said. "Maybe she has pneumonia."

"Medicine," Gracie said again.

"I heard you, Gracie," I said. "What's that pink stuff?"

"Penicillin," Gracie said. She bobbed her head like she was saying "yes" way too much.

"I hate that stuff," I said.

"It's not nice to hate," Dot said.

Mr. Edison rocked back on his heels. "We live in a wonderful time," he said. "So many modern conveniences." He waved his arms around the workroom. "Long-burning light bulbs. The phonograph.

Indoor toilets. This is the modern age. But babies still get sick. I'm sorry, Charles."

Crowe stared up at Gracie. "What did you say?" he said.

"It tastes like bad bubblegum," I said.

"Not you, George. What did the bird say?" he said.

"You mean penicillin?" I said.

Uh-oh. Had penicillin been invented yet? Something thumped in my chest.

"I received a strange letter this afternoon," Crowe said.

Gracie hopped to the edge of the cabinet. She leaned over the edge. She watched Crowe and me. Dot moved the chair closer again.

"A letter?" I said.

"It wasn't signed," Crowe said. "But it used the word *penicillin*. It said that the medicine could save Scarlett. That I should make one trip to get this miracle drug."

One trip?

Wait.

A trip in the time machine? My mouth froze open. Like a SpaghettiO.

"Danger," Gracie said. "Danger, George."

"I know, Gracie," I said. But I couldn't say a word about a time machine. To anyone.

"A miracle," Mr. Edison said. "Yes. Hope for a miracle, Charles." He clapped a hand on Crowe. "I'd like to talk more about the show tonight. We're almost ready. But the lamp factory still has to make two hundred bulbs."

"I'll get right on it, Thomas," said Crowe. He looked me right in the eye. "You and I will talk later, George."

While Mr. Edison and Crowe spoke I tried to breathe.

"Act normal, George," Gracie said. "Act normal."

Dot made a grab for Gracie. Gracie flapped her wings and landed on a pipe that stood above a worktable.

Act normal.

I could sort of do that.

I walked over to two men writing math problems on a chalkboard. A metal box sat on their table. Wires stuck out of it. One long wire was hooked to a toy train engine on a track.

"What are you doing?" I said. They kept working. Like I wasn't standing in front of them. Watching. Feeling shaky.

A letter about making one trip and penicillin?

It had to be from Old Crowe.

It had to be.

"Electricity may be the answer, William," the man with a fat mustache said.

He turned a knob on the box. Sparks flew into the air. The train engine leaped forward on the track. It crashed into a toy bridge.

"Whoa," I said, because how cool was that?

The other man wrote numbers on the board. "Not enough energy, Gene," he said. "We need the energy of a star to make that train move faster."

Gene put the train back on the track. William turned the knob. The train shot forward toward the bridge. This time it disappeared before it got there.

Gene and William did a dance. "Eureka!" said William.

I heard a crash. The train appeared again. Smashed up against the bridge.

"Curses," said Gene. He pulled on his fat mustache. "Back to the drawing board."

I couldn't believe it. "Wow. You discovered how to travel in time," I said. Only my voice was soft. And a little scared.

"Not quite, young man," said Gene. "We're so close. We need Mr. Edison to help us. But he's too busy planning his party."

I gulped. The spit got caught in the back of my throat.

It was Mr. Edison.

He had invented our time machine.

"Maybe speed of light isn't the answer," I said. "Have you looked into wormholes?"

"What's a wormhole?" Gene said. "Like fish bait? How would that help?"

"Oh, sorry," I said. "I guess wormholes haven't been discovered yet. Maybe that's Einstein."

The two men stared at me. They were like statues. With fish eyes. "You're a strange boy, aren't you?" said William.

"Hee hee, yeah. I guess so," I said. I scooted away. Before I said too much. Again.

This was not good.

Now I knew why me and Gracie came to Menlo Park.

We had to stop the two Crowes from stealing Mr. Edison's time machine.

CHAPTER 6

Bird for Sale—Cheep!

"Come here, pretty bird," Mr. Edison said. "Hurry down. We have a party to plan for."

Talking to Mr. Edison sounded pretty good. But that Dot? Not so good. She grabbed for my foot. I stepped away.

"Party?" I said.

My head did that up and down thing. It was like someone pulled a string. How embarrassing.

"George?" I flapped my wings and hollered.

"What, Gracie?" George said.

"*Little Women*," I said. My voice sounded, well, birdy.

"Right," George said.

"You are beautiful, Gracie," Mr. Edison said.

"Thank you," I said.

I flew to his shoulder and landed right by Mr. Edison's head.

Dot clapped. She smiled so big I could see she was missing two teeth.

"Father, let me hold the bird," Dot said.

Mr. Edison held his hand out for me to stand on. I moved to his palm. He stretched one of my wings out. "Fine specimen," he said. "And look at this locket. Perfect. I never thought of outfitting any of my birds with jewelry."

I bobbed my head.

Mr. Edison petted me. "Did you know, George, I haven't heard a bird sing in years? My hearing is so bad. That's great for work. It helps me concentrate. But I miss some things."

George nodded. He looked nervous.

"My hearing gets worse and worse." Mr. Edison petted my neck and shoulders.

"Gracie can't carry a tune," George said.

I would have raised my eyebrows at him. If I had eyebrows.

"I can too," I said. "I can sing great."

Grandpa and George always say to stop making that noise-like-a-donkey-is-dying when I sing with the radio.

But as a bird, a beautiful bird (the world's most famous inventor had said so), I knew this was my chance.

I crawled up to Mr. Edison's shoulder.

I cleared my throat.

"God bless America," I sang. I made sure it was loud. Real loud. "Land that I looooooove."

Dot covered her ears.

"Stand beside her."

The men working around the room looked at me.

"And guide her."

George's eyes bugged out of his head.

"Through the night with a light"—

"Stop it, Gracie," George said. "You're hurting everyone's ears."

—"from above."

Mr. Edison grinned. He threw back his head and laughed. "Amazing, Gracie. Simply amazing."

Dot said, "Father, I want the bird to go away."

I gave a bow.

Mr. Edison scooped me up. Some of the men

still stared. A few got back to their work.

"You know, George," Mr. Edison said. "I see that Gracie's pin feathers haven't been cut. A little clip and she won't be able to fly away from—"

I didn't wait for the next word. Just like that I flapped my wings. With a little jump, I was in the air. Flying.

"Yahoo," I said. "Keeping the pin feathers!"

I felt like singing. Again.

"God bless Ameeeeeer-i-ca—"

"Stop it!" Everyone in the room yelled. "Stop singing."

Mr. Edison grinned.

Crowe watched with buggy-out eyes too.

George didn't even glance at me. He's used to my singing. He rested his feet on the birdcage.

I flew around the room, looking out the windows. Looking at the lab with all its gadgets and experiments and tables. The men running. Getting ready for a party. A couple of guys played with a toy train. *Shouldn't they be working?*

Oh. I could soar. And fast.

"Gracie," George said. "We're going soon. Give it a rest. Come on down here."

I ignored George. Sometimes he thinks he's smarter than, well, Thomas Edison. Instead, I landed on a shelf. Dot stood with her hands on her hips.

Note to self: To keep Dot from touching me, sing.

Outside, snow fell, light as feathers. The grass looked like someone had sprinkled powered sugar on it. Mmmmm. Sugar. The trees shivered in the wind. The sun was hidden behind snow clouds again.

Someone hurried up to the lab the back way.

The back way?

Oh, no.

"Crowe," I said. Only it was a squawk. My little bird heart pounded.

Young Crowe let out a laugh. "Gracie has learned my name, fellows. She's a genius."

George motioned for me.

I gripped the shelf with my claws. Flapped my wings. Baby green feathers floated to the floor. Old Crowe bent against the wind. His jacket waved as he walked.

"George," Mr. Edison called, "that bird of yours is perfect."

I glanced out the window. Old Crowe was getting closer.

"I'll buy her," Mr. Edison said. "My children will love her. Dot, don't you love Gracie?"

"Not anymore," Dot said. "She hurt my ears. She sings awful."

"I think she would be a great family pet," Mr. Edison said.

George shook his head. "My sister would kill me," he said.

Mr. Edison nodded. "That's too bad. She'd be a welcome addition."

Old Crowe left tracks in the snow.

"Crowe!" I said again. My shoulders moved up and down. "Warning! Danger! God bless America!"

We had to get out of here. Or at least lock the doors.

Mr. Edison laughed. "I bet your sister loves that bird," he said.

"She sure does," George said. "A lot."

"Crowe!" This time my parrot voice was loud. Real loud.

"That's becoming annoying," said Young Crowe. He folded his arms.

George stood. "Crowe?" he said. "You mean our Crowe?"

"Yes," I said.

"Come here, Gracie," he said. He grabbed hold of the birdcage. His knuckles were white.

Then he talked fast.

"Mr. Edison," George said. "I have a package for you. It's a book you signed for my grandpa. It's called *Little Women*."

"Yes, I remember your grandfather," Mr. Edison said. "He was here a while back. With a young woman who carried a garter snake in her carpet bag."

Mom and Dad.

I'd almost forgotten that we came to save them.

George patted one side of his jacket. His eyes grew big.

He patted his other side.

I settled on his shoulder and pecked his head a good one.

I knew where this was going.

Old Crowe was just outside the door.

And now this.

The silly human I called a brother had lost the book.

CHAPTER 7

The Wrong Crowe

Things were going from bad to worse.

Old Crowe writing a letter to himself.

Young Crowe watching us close.

And now I had lost *Little Women*.

I had to find that book.

Me and Gracie were supposed to give it to some-one in 1879. Anyone.

Wet might be okay. But lost sure wasn't.

"What is it, George?" said Mr. Edison. "What are you looking for?"

"*Little Women*," I said. I felt under my hat. Inside my coat.

"Speak louder," he said. He moved closer.

This time I hollered. "*Little Women.*"

Mr. Edison chuckled. "How little are these women?"

"No, the book," I said. I didn't feel like laughing right then.

"This is no time for teasing, Thomas," said Crowe. "I think the boy's worried."

Crowe took the birdcage out of my hand. He looked inside. "Nothing in here, George. Where'd you have it last?"

Sweat popped up on my upper lip. "In the buggy, I think. I don't remember."

I hit my head to wake up my brain. I looked on the bottom of my shoe. Like the book would be there or something.

"We can't go home unless we return it," I said.

"Oh dear," Crowe said. "This is serious. I don't know what I would do if I couldn't get home to my family."

He walked to the front doors. He eyed the floor as he walked. "We start by retracing our steps. Do just what you did before. I'll be back." He walked right out the doors. Into the snow.

Carrying our time machine.

Now what?

Cold air swirled in the room.

Dot watched Gracie. "I like the bird when she doesn't sing." She reached for Gracie.

Gracie hummed "God Bless America" again.

Dot howled. She hid behind Mr. Edison's legs.

Gracie perched on a shelf. "George. Go get the time machine." She pointed with a wing.

Lucky for her Mr. Edison couldn't hear her talk like a girl. Instead of a bird, I mean.

I wanted to cry but I didn't.

"Don't you worry, my boy," Mr. Edison said. He patted my shoulder. "We'll all help you find your book."

"I can help," Dot said. "I'm a good helper."

Mr. Edison climbed up on a table. He cupped both hands around his mouth and yelled, "Attention, everyone. Your attention."

Each man stopped his work to look up. The room went quiet. No more clanking and banging. No more burning stuff in test tubes. No more scratching math problems on paper.

Gracie cocked her head to the side and watched Mr. Edison.

"This young man has lost a book," he said. He

bent down toward me. "What color is it, George?"

"Brown," I said.

"The book is titled *Little Women*," he said to the lab assistants. "It has a brown cover. I need each of you to take a break now. Please see if you can't find this novel. We know it is not in this room."

Mr. Edison's assistants pulled on their coats. They went out the front doors after Young Crowe. They laughed and talked on the way out.

Gene messed up my hair when he walked by me. He winked.

"Maybe one of your wormholes ate the book," Gene said.

William laughed.

"We'll find it, George," Gracie said.

I breathed deep. "I hope so," I said.

I heard a door open.

Crowe walked into the lab.

Through the back door.

Without the birdcage.

Or the book.

He looked at me. Then at Gracie.

"Awk! Run, George," Gracie said.

"Nevermore," she squawked. "Nevermore."

"What's that supposed to mean?" I said. I stared up at her.

She rested on another pipe.

Her neck feathers stood straight up. Her wings opened partway.

"What's the matter with you?" I said.

"Nevermore," she said again. A few feathers floated to the floor. Then something else dropped onto the floor from under Gracie's tail feathers. It was white and not so nice.

"Yuck," I said, staring at the dropping.

"Pardon me," Gracie said.

Mr. Edison hopped down from the table. "'Nevermore' is from 'The Raven.' It's a long poem about death."

"Yes, Gracie is a genius too, isn't she?" said Crowe. He put his hand on my shoulder. "Hello, George."

A cold wind followed him.

It froze me clear to my bones.

This was the wrong Crowe.

"Oh. Hello, Charles," said Mr. Edison. He took out his pocket watch. "You weren't gone long. Did you find it?"

"Yes, sir. I believe I have found what I was searching for." His hand tightened on me.

"George and Gracie and I need to have a little talk."

"Awk!" said Gracie. She walked back and forth along the pipe.

My stomach walked back and forth too.

"Splendid," said Mr. Edison. "I'll leave you to it." He took his coat off a hook. "The boys and I are off to the lamp factory. The town is counting on a grand New Year's Eve electric spectacular. I'd hate to disappoint them." He rubbed his hands together.

He plopped his hat on his head. "After all, genius is one percent inspiration and ninety-nine percent perspiration." He took Dot's hand and hurried out the front doors.

"Wait," I said. But Old Crowe squeezed my shoulder tighter.

He pulled me to the back of the laboratory. My legs shook so bad I couldn't walk. Crowe drug me along.

"Where is the time machine?" he said through gritted teeth.

Nobody was around to help me. Except for Gracie. And she was just a little parrot.

"I don't know," I said. Which was sort of a lie because Young Crowe had it. Somewhere outside. No way would I tell *him* that.

"Make this easy, George," he said. "Don't make

trouble for yourself. Or for Gracie."

I swallowed. "Nevermore," I said.

That's when Gracie dove from the ceiling. Right at Crowe's head. She grabbed at his hair.

"Get him, Gracie," I said. I pushed and kicked. Crowe held on tight to my arm.

Gracie dove again. Crowe ducked. He slapped at her. But he missed.

Gracie could fly fast. For a girl.

"Let go of George," she said with a squawk.

"Help!" I yelled. Who would hear me, though?

I kicked and wiggled to get free. Crowe was too strong. He pulled me out the back door. He slammed it shut.

Gracie flew to the window. She knocked knocked knocked the glass with her beak.

She couldn't get out.

She couldn't help me.

Crowe put his face close to mine. "Tell me where the time machine is, George. Then you and Gracie can go home."

My heart banged inside my rib cage. "I know what you want to do," I said. I breathed in the cold. The air cleared my head. "Now that you're back home, you'll break the time machine. Me and Gracie will never see our parents or Grandpa again." I yanked my arm away. "I won't tell you anything."

Crowe's face was angry.

I stood there, tall as I could.

Crowe stepped back.

"It doesn't matter," he said. His voice was almost a whisper. "I know where another one is."

He tipped his hat to me. "Race you home, George," he said. He ran off down the boardwalk.

My shoulders slumped. I shivered in the cold.

"George," Gracie said from inside the laboratory. She sounded like she had a cup over her beak. She knocked on the window again. "Where's he going?"

I swallowed.

My legs got weak all of a sudden.

"He knows where another time machine is," I said.

No.

I threw open the door and ran into the building. "He's going to break the time machine, Gracie." I almost couldn't get the words out. "The one that Mr. Edison is inventing. Right now."

Gracie flew from the window to my shoulder. She put her beak on my nose.

"Mr. Edison invented a time machine?" she said.

"Not *a* time machine," I said. "*Our* time machine." I paced back and forth. "Don't you get it?"

"Ye—maybe," Gracie said. "No. I don't get it." She rubbed her head on her wing.

"No time. I'll tell you on the way," I said. "Come on." I raced out to the front yard. Gracie flew along above me.

The sky was gray. The snow had stopped falling. But the wind blew ice crystals at my cheeks.

"Can you see Mr. Edison, Gracie?" I said.

"Over there," she said.

She flew toward some trees. Right where Mr. Edison and Dot and the assistants walked.

I hollered, "Mr. Edison!"

Mr. Edison stopped. "George," he said. "Have you found *Little Women*?"

I shook my head no.

"Gracie would like to play with Dot." I said the words fast because that was all I could think of.

"Stupid, George," Gracie said. She sounded like the real Gracie this time. Not bird Gracie. And that can be scary.

Dot jumped up and down. "Can I play with the birdy, Father?" She said it loud. "If she doesn't sing?"

"Of course, my dear," said Mr. Edison. "Go on home, Dot. Show George and Gracie the way." Mr.

Edison pointed. "Now where's Charles gotten off to?"

"He said something about a note," said William. His voice was loud and deep. "He said he needed to meet with someone."

I let out a big breath because I didn't know what to tell him about Crowe. The old one or the young one. Except me and Gracie were in lots of trouble.

"Have fun, kids." Mr. Edison slapped me on the back.

Then he followed his assistants until they disappeared into the trees. I guess toward the lamp factory.

Dot looked at Gracie all shy.

"Are you crazy, George?" Gracie said. "You-Know-Who will squeeze me like a catsup bottle. You better tell me what's going on. Right now."

"I think Old Crowe is there," I said. "At Mr. Edison's house."

Dot grabbed my hand. "I'll show you the way," she said.

"I hate that guy, George," said Gracie.

"It's not nice to hate," said Dot. She frowned at Gracie.

"Sorry," said Gracie. "What I meant to say is,

that guy is mean. He needs a spanking."

"Okay," said Dot. She pulled me down the boardwalk.

"What's your plan, George?" said Gracie.

"Old Crowe left a letter for Young Crowe," I said. "He told him about traveling to the future. To get penicillin for Scarlett."

We had caused so much trouble. Especially for Mom and Dad.

I closed my eyes. "Now both Crowes are after the time machine."

"And we don't even have the book. What do we do, George?" Gracie said. She looked scared—for a bird.

I took a deep breath of the cold air. When I let it out, a cloud hovered right over Gracie.

"We have to save the time machine. And you and me. And Mom and Dad," I said. "And maybe even both Crowes. Before those two make the dumbest mistake ever."

"Great plan," she said.

"Yup, great plan," Dot said.

"How do we do all that?" Gracie asked.

I gulped. "I don't know."

Because I wasn't so sure we could do any of it.

CHAPTER 8

Time after Time . . . Again

So here we were. Stuck.

Really stuck.

Out in the cold. With a little girl who might squeeze my head off.

Without *Little Women*.

And both time machines missing.

Plus, the really scary part—two Crowes. Also both missing.

Sure, flying was everything I thought it might be. Even more.

I could go fast. And high.

I could see who was where. Even the bad guys.

I could even drop surprise packages—all accidental—on the crowd below.

But I didn't want to stay like this forever. I wanted to go home.

We had to give that book away. We had to stop both Crowes. We had to get our time machine and get back to Grandpa. Now.

"Old Crowe, Young Crowe," George said. "Where are they?" I could tell by his voice he was thinking. Hard. His eyes had gone crossed a little.

Dot skipped down the wooden sidewalk. "Old Crowe. Young Crowe," she said. Her voice was sing-songy.

Wind whistled past. Even in the olden days it was cold. Maybe even colder than back home.

At least in our day, I had a coat to wear when it snowed. Not feathers.

"We got some big problems here, Gracie," George said.

"I'll say," I said.

"I'll say," Dot said. She had a pretty good singing voice. "I'll say."

Except she sounded like a parrot.

"We know Old Crowe will try to destroy the time machine."

"De-stroy. De-stroy. Deeeeeee-stroooooy." Now Dot stomped along.

I flew above them, just higher than George's head.

"Plus Young Crowe has the birdcage time machine," I said. "And you don't know where he is. Do you? Do you?"

Dot watched us.

George looked guilty. "That's not my fault," he said.

"I know, George," I said.

A blanket of snow settled on my beak.

"Get a move on, George. Birds usually fly south for winter."

"That's where I live," Dot said. She pointed to the house at the end of the boardwalk.

"Right," George said. He looked around. "Do you see Crowe anywhere, Gracie?"

"Which one?" I said.

"He's probably in the cellar," Dot said. She swiped her nose with her sleeve.

George stopped walking. "What?" he said.

I flew in front of Dot. "What do you mean?" I said.

"Charles works in there. On Father's secret invention." Dot's cheeks were pink with cold. I landed on her shoulder.

"Hello, Dot," I said. "Pretty girl."

"No singing," she said. She pointed right at my eyeball.

"She won't sing, Dot," George said. "If you'll take us to the cellar."

"All right."

Dot led us to the back of the house. She opened a door. Stairs went into a basement.

"It's dark down there," I said. "Dark."

"Scary," George said. Only he whispered the word.

"It's not scary in the room," Dot said. "Father works down here sometimes. I come with him."

We eased down the steps.

Opened the door.

The room was full of light. A table ran along one wall. A workbench that reminded me of Grandpa was pushed against the other wall. There was a phonograph in the corner. Several tube thingys were stacked on the table beside the machine.

"This looks like a room from our museum," George said. He turned to look at me.

"Mom and Dad were here." We both said it at the same time.

I wanted to say jinx, but I couldn't get the word out.

"Getting the best stuff from the past," I said.

Just like that, I missed our parents more than anything. We had to get home. Then go to the next state. And the next. "This is taking too long, George. We have to hurry. We have to help Mom and Dad."

Crowe stepped from a dark corner.

"Charles!" Dot said. She ran to him and gave him a hug. I fluttered into the air and landed on George's head.

Which Charles was he? Old or young? Mean or nice?

"Good to see you two together," Crowe said. He moved closer to George. "Now. Where is the time machine?"

Great. The mean guy.

George backed up. "I don't know."

Before I could say "None of your business," a slow whine came from another corner. Several loud pops filled the air. Something shimmered, lighting up the space.

"Father's coming," Dot said.

There was a BANG! A puff of smoke. I flapped my wings. George said, "Erp!" and gave a jump.

Mr. Edison sat before us on a fancy chair. He held onto a lever with one hand. The lever was hooked to the chair leg. In his other hand he held the birdcage. "Still needs a little work," he said. Then, "Dot! George and Gracie. Charles. What are you all doing here?"

"Waiting for you, Thomas," Crowe said.

Mr. Edison beamed. "So you see my newest experiment, George and Gracie. I'm exploring time travel."

George nodded and I slid forward on his head.

"Charles, why are *you* here?" Mr. Edison stood and walked to George and me. "If you were going to see the children, why did you send me to give them this?"

Mr. Edison handed George the birdcage. It trembled and glowed.

Crowe stepped closer to George. "I'll take that," he said.

But George put the cage behind his back. "It's ours," he said. "You can't have it."

George looked like he might cry.

I tried to growl and scare Crowe away. And snarl.

And roar like a lion. But I only got a "Yaaaack!" to come out.

"God Bless America" would have been more scary.

Crowe narrowed his eyes at me. He smiled with thin lips.

Which gave me the creeps.

"So what do you think of my newest invention?" Mr. Edison patted the chair. Wires and knobs stuck out everywhere. "Charles has been working on this with me. And some of the boys in the shop."

"It's great," George said. But he sounded like he didn't mean it.

"Father and I ride back and forth to the Invention Factory," Dot said. She skipped over to Mr. Edison. "And sometimes to town. Don't we?"

"Yes we do," Mr. Edison said. He lifted his daughter in a hug. "Saves time."

"So that's how you disappeared so fast this morning," George said.

I said, "Can it go more than to the lab or to town? Like to the future? Or backward to the past?"

Mr. Edison opened his mouth. Then he closed it. He looked at Crowe. And Dot. Then he said, "Perhaps, Gracie. But pushing time too far in any direction can be a dangerous thing."

My birdy blood pounded in my ears. Maybe we could stop things now. Right here. Maybe, if there was no time machine, everything would be back to the way it was. Mom and Dad would be home. Like in the movies when everything gets fixed before the end.

"Tell Mr. Edison, George," I said. "Warn him."

Mr. Edison dusted off the chair. That time machine didn't rattle or roll or glow or anything like ours does.

"You have to make rules for your machine, Mr. Edison," said George. "Like you can't steal stuff when you ride in it. Or . . . or buy stuff either . . . Or or . . ."

"Or change into animals," I said.

Mr. Edison put his hand on George's head. "I'm only the inventor, George," he said. "I don't control the rules of time. I don't even know what they are yet. That's what makes time travel dangerous. Not knowing."

"Now, Thomas," Crowe said. "George has a wonderful imagination. But he's only a child. Gracie is a bird, for heaven's sake. You have work to do. A celebration to get ready for."

"The children have given me an idea, Charles." Mr. Edison settled himself at a work desk. He took out paper and pen and jotted down some notes. "Yes. The boy and the bird have got me thinking. Dot, run upstairs to Mother. Tell her I won't be in all day."

"Yes, Father," Dot said. She hurried away.

"Charles," Mr. Edison said. "You have work to do too. Here. I need you hanging lights. Then you must go to your Scarlett."

I looked at Crowe.

Crowe was sad.

He couldn't go to Scarlett.

He was trying to fix things.

Like us.

"I'll meet up with you two soon," Crowe said. He left the room the same way Dot had.

"Charles is acting strange," Mr. Edison said. He wrote more notes. Tapped his finger on his lips. Then he got up and went to the time machine chair. He adjusted knobs. Re-connected wires. He wound a crank like the one on the phonograph. It came off in his hand.

He said, "There are a few kinks left. Over time, I'll work them out."

Crowe ran down the stairs and into the room again.

"Bwak!" I said. "He's back."

"George. Gracie." he said. He got to us in two steps. Crowe knelt in front of George. "Scarlett's worse. Tell me what you know about penicillin."

"Young Crowe," I said. "Young."

"The letter said to watch out for a girl or a boy, new to town. And a talking animal." Crowe looked at me. "You're a talking animal, aren't you, Gracie?"

I gulped.

"I guess so," I said.

"Charles. Please. Back to work." Mr. Edison said. But Crowe didn't answer him.

"Tell me about the medicine," Crowe said. He sounded afraid.

I could hear George gulp.

"It makes sick people get better," George said.

"I need to get to the future," said Crowe.

"What did you say, Charles?" Mr. Edison said.

Crowe pulled a book from his jacket. "Here's *Little Women*," he said and gave it to George. Crowe ran to the time machine chair.

He sat in it. Locked a seat belt. Pushed the lever forward.

"Charles, no . . . not the future," said Mr. Edison. He dove for the chair.

And with a WHOOSH! Young Crowe was gone.

CHAPTER 9

Something Fishy

Our birdcage time machine shook. It quivered. It sort of glowed. And spun around.

"Oh my," said Mr. Edison.

Then WHOOSH! our time machine was gone too.

It disappeared. Right out of my hands.

"What the heck?" is all I could say. Because . . . *What the heck?* Our time machine left. Without me and Gracie.

"Awk! That's our ride home," Gracie said. She dug her claws into my head. She whined like a parrot. Because she still was one. Maybe forever now.

My mouth hung open. Like the giant's mouth at the miniature golf course back home.

Mr. Edison scratched his head. "Dear, dear," he said. "I didn't expect that. Not at all." He stared at me. Then at Gracie.

"You kids aren't from around here. Are you?" He poked my shoulder. He poked at Gracie too. I could feel her sliding in my hair.

Gracie bobbed up and down. "Nevermore," she said, which I think meant "No, we are not from around here."

I shook my head. Gracie slipped off my head and onto my shoulder. "Watch it, George," she said.

I handed Mr. Edison *Little Women*. "This is for you," I said. "From my grandpa."

"I see," Mr. Edison said, taking the book. He went back to his desk. "I hadn't thought about the future overlapping the present." He scribbled something on notepaper.

"What happened to our birdcage?" I said.

"Now, George," Mr. Edison said. "Let's be honest. That's no ordinary birdcage. It's my machine, isn't it?"

"I don't know if it's yours," I said. "It's from the future. Where me and Gracie live. At least"—I swallowed—"we used to live there."

"Don't give up yet," said Mr. Edison. "We'll get you and Gracie back home. Where you belong."

"Our parents are lost too," Gracie said. "That's why we're here. To help them."

"I see," Mr. Edison said.

I hoped he really *did* see because I didn't.

"We can figure this out," Mr. Edison said.

Gracie cocked her head to the right.

Mr. Edison cocked his head to the right. "The machines are stuck together like magnets. What would make them do that?"

Gracie cocked her head to the left.

Mr. Edison cocked his head to the left

They're both strange birds. If you ask me.

"What if Crowe doesn't come back with our time machine, George?" Gracie said. "How will we get home?"

I sat on the floor and rested my head in my hands. I was scared. We were stuck in 1879. So Mom and Dad were stuck too. For good. Grandpa would be all alone. "I don't know what to do, Gracie." My throat was tight. From trying not to cry.

Gracie put a wing on my shoulder. "We'll think of something, George," she said.

"Maybe I can help," said Mr. Edison. "Let me do some figuring."

He looked up at the ceiling.

He felt around on the floor where the time machine had been.

He wrote more notes.

He pulled his watch out of his pocket. It hung from a chain. "It's getting late. Everyone will arrive soon. For the New Year's Eve light show. We must hurry."

He frowned at me and Gracie.

Then he wrote one last time. He stood up from his desk and slid the chair in.

"I gotta think too, Gracie," I said.

"I'll help," said Gracie. She buried her head in her wing.

"Does that work?" I said.

"I don't know yet." Gracie sounded like she had a sock in her mouth.

I tried but I didn't get any ideas. Then my brain sort of buzzed. And sparked. And whirred. And lit up the room.

Wait a second. Lit up the room?

That wasn't my brain.

WHOOSH! Young Crowe was back. All squished

up in a smoking fish tank. With no water.

BAM! A revolving door appeared. All shiny. It landed so close to my face that my nose touched it.

"Is that you, Time Machine?" I said. I knocked on the glass door.

The time machine shivered.

Mr. Edison smiled so his teeth showed. "How wonderful. The machine changes shape when it travels through time. And it has a personality." He wrote that in his notebook too.

"You came back," Gracie said so loud that I said "Ouch, Gracie," and covered my ears.

She spread her wings. And hugged the revolving door.

Our time machine shivered again.

Crowe climbed out of the fish tank. Crowe's coat had smoke coming off it. He held out several pink plastic medicine bottles. "I found the medicine. It took me two days. And I had to escape the authorities. But I got it."

"The penicillin," Gracie said. Her voice was quiet. "Oh, no. He stole it, George."

"I know, Gracie," I said. A tiny light of an idea lit up in my brain.

Crowe laughed like a crazy guy. He jumped

around the room. "The future is everything, Thomas." He grabbed Mr. Edison by the shoulders. "Why have you never gone there yourself? People don't die from a little cough in the future. They travel through the air in flying machines. They go to the moon in rocket ships. Think of it. Do you want to see into the future, Thomas? I'll show you. Everyone owns your electric lights. How magnificent it all is."

That light in my brain got bigger.

"Charles," said Mr. Edison. His forehead wrinkled. "What have you done?"

"What have I done, Thomas? Do you mean, what will I do?" He stopped jumping around. He narrowed his eyes. He put his face right in Mr. Edison's. "The answer is . . . everything. The best part is that I will do it all before you."

He looked like Old Crowe. Which gave me the shivers.

"The world will call *me* the genius. *I* will be 'the Wizard of the World.'"

"I like 'the Wizard of Menlo Park' better," said Gracie. "Ack!"

Crowe didn't even look at Gracie. "First I will heal my little Scarlett. Because, at last, now I can." He ran to the stairs.

Mr. Edison followed behind him. "Traveling in time is dangerous, Charles," he said. "You must never visit the future again."

My brain lit up like a campfire. I knew how Crowe got stuck to the time machine. He broke all the rules of Time. Every single one, I bet.

"He's nutso," said Gracie.

I nodded. "For sure."

Crowe opened the cellar door and ran outside.

Cold air blew down on us. I could see stars in the night sky.

Mr. Edison turned to me and Gracie. "Listen to me, children," he said. He didn't crack a smile. "I don't know exactly why you're here in 1879. But if Charles takes my machine to the future again, you will never get home. Do you understand?"

My stomach kerplunked. "I do," I said.

Gracie blinked. "Me too," she said. "Me too."

"Don't start that again," I said.

She gulped. "Okay," she said. "I'm better."

"Why is our time machine stuck to yours, Mr. Edison?" I said. "It never was before. I don't think."

"No, it wasn't, George," he said. "Something has changed to cause this to happen. What could it be?"

I looked at Gracie.

She looked at me.

"What did you do, George?" she said.

"It wasn't me," I said. I wasn't sure though. Maybe because I lost *Little Women*?

"Perhaps it was me." Old Crowe stepped out of a dark corner. He held a stick.

"Charles?" said Mr. Edison. He peered at Crowe. "I saw you leave just now . . . A-a-a-h. You're from the future."

"Not him again," I said.

"Nice to see you too, George," said Old Crowe.

"Oh boy, oh boy," said Gracie.

"You don't have to be afraid, Gracie. I've come to help," Crowe said. He held the stick with both hands.

"Not if I can help it," said Gracie. She flew up and landed on top of our time machine.

Mr. Edison raised his eyebrows. "You've caused all of this trouble, Charles. Somehow you've gotten yourself tied to these machines. So they're tied together when you're close by."

"I'm here to help," Crowe said. "To fix everything."

Mr. Edison stepped in front of the fish tank. "What could you possibly do to help, Charles?"

"Don't trust him, Mr. Edison," I said. "He wants to break the time machine. Both of them."

"I only want to destroy that one." Crowe pointed to the fish tank. "That will free George and Gracie's parents. And me. Before Charles . . . before I make a foolish mistake and return to the future. A second time."

"Wait, wait," said Gracie. She sounded like a police siren. "You can't. If you break Mr. Edison's machine, you'll break ours too." She paced along the top of the revolving door.

"A chance I will have to take," said Crowe. He leaped forward, the stick raised.

Mr. Edison dove into the fish tank. "You have to find it first," he said. He pulled the lever backward. And WHOOSH! he was gone.

WHOOSH! Our time machine was gone too.

"Stupid man," said Crowe. His face turned red. He looked at me and Gracie. "Don't fret, children. You may enjoy living here with me."

He rushed up the stairs and outside.

Before I could even blink, I heard a popping sound. The room lit up. WHOOSH! In a puff of smoke, there was Mr. Edison.

Sitting in the fish tank. Again.

But our time machine wasn't with him.

"George and Gracie," he said, climbing out of the tank. "Your machine is outside behind the lamp factory. Hidden beneath a covering." He held out his hand. "Hurry, children. You can ride over in my machine."

Gracie flew down to him. "Come on, George," she said. "What are you waiting for?"

"It's still smoking," I said. "Plus it smells." I held my nose.

"Get in here, George," said Gracie in a dangerous voice. "Now."

I didn't wait one more second.

Mr. Edison boosted me inside. Gracie hopped on my shoulder.

"Do *not* let Charles find you with my machine," said Mr. Edison. "That will be disastrous for all of you."

Gracie nodded. Or else she was bobbing again. I couldn't tell the difference.

Mr. Edison looked at his watch. "My guests are arriving even as we speak. I'll be here at the light show if you need me. I'll watch for Charles too."

Mr. Edison pulled the lever back. He set it for 11:45 p.m.

"Hey," I said. "You set the time for right this second."

"Traveling forward—or backward—in time is dangerous, George," he said.

Then WHOOSH! we were sucked into a black hole.

CHAPTER 10

Eenie Meenie Miney Mo

Thunk!

"That didn't take long," I said. I fluttered around in the fish tank.

"We didn't go anywhere," George said. "Only across the yard."

I stepped on his face and hopped away into the cold. We were in the back of a building, like Mr. Edison said. Right by a woodpile was our time machine, the revolving door. Under a cover.

"I see our machine," I said.

George seemed to be stuck. But after a little shimmy he broke free of the tank.

"I guess when you move sideways in time—not into the future or past—the machine doesn't change shape," George said.

"Good and not good," I said. "Means both Crowes know what they're looking for."

George's breath was a cloud when he spoke. "Mr. Edison has the book now. That means we can go home."

"We better do it, quick," I said. "You know both Crowes are looking for us. And these." I pointed with my feathers at the time machine.

"Hey George? Gracie?" Dot ran down the boardwalk, her coat flapping in the night air. "Come see what Father has done. It's beautiful."

Dot grabbed George's hand and pulled him along.

"Wait, Dot," George said. "We have to go home."

"Everyone is here," she said. "Everyone in the whole world. You have to see too."

George and Dot crunched through the snow. They walked around the corner of the building. I followed them down Christie Street.

All around us were lights. Strung here and there. On the buildings. Along the street. In the frozen trees.

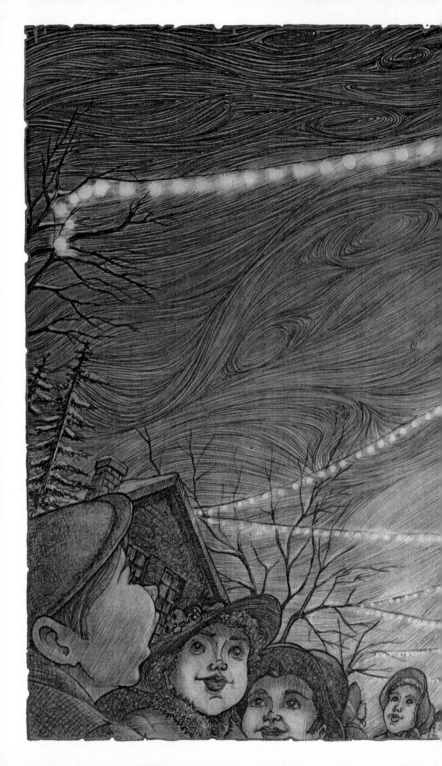

It was like Christmas.

The lights reflected in the snow.

They reflected in the windowpanes of the houses and buildings. "Listen to them," I said.

"Who?" George said.

"All these people."

There were people at the train depot. Women in dresses that swept the ground. Men in suits. Mr. Edison laughed. Horses pulling buggies clip-clopped along the icy street. Kids ran outside.

And everyone, everyone oohed and aaahed.

What must it be like to have no indoor light at all? I mean, nothing more than a candle? And now, here it was. All of it. Lights for everyone. Lights anyone could buy.

"This is the most beautifulest night ever," Dot said.

Mr. Edison saw us. He hurried over.

"You two are still here?" he said.

Dot swung from George's hand. "These are my friends," she said.

"They have to leave," Mr. Edison said. "I just saw Charles. He's looking for the device."

"Charles is over at the lamp factory," Dot said. "I saw him when we were leaving."

I didn't wait to hear anything more. "Hurry," I said to George. "Goodbye, Dot. Goodbye, Mr. Edison."

George ran. I flew ahead of him.

"No!" I said all squawky.

Young Crowe stood at the fish tank.

"George. Gracie." he said. "You can't stop me. I've seen what the future holds. I'm going back for more."

"No," George said. "You can't. If you steal from Time . . ."

But George didn't even get to finish his sentence.

"I'll make a few adjustments," Young Crowe said. He climbed inside the fish tank. "Fix this little machine right up when I'm in a more modern time with more modern tools. I'll be back for my family. I'll carry them to the future too. So we can stay there together. And everyone will know Charles Crowe. The Wizard of the World."

Hot air swirled around the fish tank. The snow melted. Lights that looked like the ones hung on Christie Street lit up the time machine. It was beautiful.

Mr. Edison ran toward me and Gracie and Charles Crowe. On the streets, people admired the lights and waited for a new year to start. A new year with lights for everybody's houses.

"Please," I said. "Our mom and dad, Mr. Crowe. Please help us get our mom and dad." I landed on George's head. "They've been gone for two years."

"Charles," Mr. Edison said. He yelled.

Out front, people cheered.

Seconds of the old year remained and Charles Crowe was taking the time machine right in front of us.

There was movement under the white tarp and then the cover flew off the revolving door. Like a merry-go-round, the door spun in slow motion. The glass changed colors every time it swung around. Blue. Pale pink. Bright yellow.

"Pretty," Dot said.

There was a bang and then, just like before, Young Crowe was gone.

The fish tank too. All that was left was a place on the ground where the snow had melted.

"No."

George and I turned.

Old Crowe stood behind Mr. Edison. He shook his head. Closed his eyes.

"No," he said again. "I left him a letter. I said not

to go back except for the medicine." Crowe pointed at us. "If you'd stayed out of my way, this wouldn't have happened. I could have stopped him."

Our time machine hummed. The lights flashed.

"We tried to stop *you*," I said. I watched the revolving door turn. Would it leave without us?

"You want power," George said. He took a step back. Toward our time machine.

"No," Crowe said. "I want my family."

For a minute I thought he might cry.

"We do too," I said. "We want Mom and Dad. We want to live with Grandpa in our museum."

A cold breeze, with just a hint of warmth, blew past us.

"They've been gone for two years," George said. "It's all your fault." George took another step back.

Mr. Edison had the book. We could go home now. If we could get to the time machine before Crowe.

When Crowe spoke he was angry. "I have been gone from my home for more than a hundred years. Everyone I know is dead and gone."

Dot let out a little gasp.

I clutched at my locket.

"Now Charles," Mr. Edison said. "Come with

me. Let's check on Scarlett. See how she's doing. Perhaps that medicine will indeed save her life."

Crowe swung toward Mr. Edison. "I've tried to see them. I've tried to get close to them. But I can't. Time won't allow it."

"Maybe I can intervene. Maybe I can bring a message to your family," said Mr. Edison.

"I'll never see them again," Crowe said. He dropped the stick he carried. His whole body sagged.

"Happy New Year," someone called, and the crowd answered, "Happy New Year!" There was cheering and clapping. The sky where we were was dark as spilled ink.

Crowe covered his face with his hands.

"Into the machine, George, Gracie," Mr. Edison said. His voice was low. He guided George toward the door. Every time it swung around there was a whoosh sound and a blast of warm air blew out at us. The snow turned red. Then green. Then purple. "You need to go now."

Dot grabbed her father's hand.

Crowe didn't move.

I flew to the revolving door. I tried not to think of Crowe and Scarlett. I tried to think only of Grandpa. And Mom and Dad.

If I closed my eyes I might be able to imagine them waiting for us.

George grabbed for me. He clutched me under his arm. "On three we go back home," he said. He looked at me. "You ready, Gracie?"

I nodded. "Okay," I said.

"One . . ." George said.

"Two," I said.

"No," Crowe said. He lunged as George stepped closer to the glass that showed all three of us like a mirror. "I will not leave my home again!"

"Three!" George said.

He jumped and for a moment it felt like I was falling down the rabbit hole in *Alice in Wonderland*. Then seat belts snaked out and slid around my waist.

I looked through the glass.

Mr. Edison held Crowe by the jacket.

And there.

There beside Mr. Edison.

"George. Gracie," a woman said. Her hair was done up. She wore a long garter snake around her neck like a scarf. Her dress touched the ground. The snake's tale waved in the wind.

Mom.

And Dad.

I made to climb out of the time machine. But the seat belt was too tight.

Instead, I waved as hard as I could. A green feather floated off and away. Mom blew a kiss. Me and George slipped farther away from her.

Then ZOOM! we were in a black hole.

CHAPTER 11

Next Stop—Home

Coming home was different from last time.

Me and Gracie spun around in the revolving door.

Back toward the future. And Grandpa.

I heard music. Like at the carnival. We twirled in slow motion.

Gracie the parrot rode by me. On a blue horse. She bobbed up and down and up and down.

"Hey, George," she said and disappeared into the dark.

Weird.

I sat in a wooden merry-go-round sled. I waved at Gracie when she and her horse came around again.

She had turned back into her girl self.

She waved a feather at me. "I smell popcorn," she said.

And disappeared.

Light bulbs glowed above our heads.

The music stopped.

BANG BUMP BANG BANG BUMP

The time machine landed in the museum. Right outside Grandpa's fix-it shop door.

"George. Gracie." Grandpa ran out of his shop. He climbed up on the time machine.

It had changed into a merry-go-round.

"That's a super cool disguise," I said.

The time machine blinked its lights.

Gracie still sat on the blue horse. "We did it, Grandpa," she said. "We left the book with Mr. Edison." She held her arms out. "I look like a plucked chicken."

"You mean a plucked parrot," I said. I giggled. I couldn't stop. Because I was funny. And because I was back home in our warm museum. Plus I had on my own clothes.

"Hilarious," said Gracie. She rubbed her arms and smiled. A lot.

"Did you miss us, Grandpa?" I said.

"You were only gone a couple of seconds," Grandpa said. He hugged Gracie. And helped her climb off the horse. "But yes. I missed you both. I was worried about you."

I jumped out of the wooden merry-go-round sled. An envelope fell out after me. I picked it up.

"What do you have there, George?" Grandpa said.

I looked at it. "It's a letter, I think. With mine and Gracie's names on the front," I said.

I walked over to Gracie and Grandpa. We stood on the merry-go-round. Grandpa leaned against a metal pole.

I opened the letter. Gracie read out loud. Over my shoulder.

My Dear Children,

Thank you for showing me that my machine works. In return, I will tell you a secret: You will bring your parents home someday. I have seen it. Remember that genius is one percent inspiration and ninety-nine percent perspiration. So keep trying.

And be careful.

Your friend, Thomas A. Edison

P.S. Tell your grandfather thank you for the book.

"Well, what do you know about that," said

Grandpa. "Mr. Edison traveled to the future. I wonder if that's how he came up with all his great invention ideas."

I shook my head. "He wouldn't do that," I said. "He likes to think up his own ideas."

"How could he, anyway? Young Crowe stole his time machine," said Gracie.

The three of us stepped off the merry-go-round. It burped.

"Young Crowe?" Grandpa said. He frowned. "Who's Young Crowe?"

"Gracie," I said. I grabbed her arm. "What if Mr. Edison built another time machine. A better one. After you and me left Menlo Park."

"So that's how he traveled to the future?" Gracie's eyes got as bright as one of Mr. Edison's light bulbs. "He saw Mom and Dad come home."

"We can do this, Gracie," I said.

"Kids," said Grandpa. He put his hands on our heads. "Who is Young Crowe?"

"It's a long story," Gracie said.

taptap tap-tap taptap tap-tap

We all three walked toward the sound. The telegraph sat in the corner of the fix-it shop.

taptap tap-tap taptap tap-tap

"Mom and Dad," Gracie said. Her voice was quiet.

"You'd think they heard us talking about them," said Grandpa.

We all rushed to the telegraph.

Grandpa grabbed his pad and pencil. He wrote the words. "Happy New Year . . . George . . . and Gracie."

The telegraph went quiet.

"Happy New Year?" Grandpa shook his head. "It's not New Year's Day."

I smiled at Gracie. "It is in 1879."

"You mean 1880 now," Gracie said.

"Oh yeah," I said. "Tell them Happy New Year back."

"Say we love them," said Gracie. She held her locket tight in her hand.

Grandpa typed the message. "Happy . . . New Year . . . We love . . . you . . . Where . . . are . . . you now?"

But the telegraph didn't answer.

"What's wrong, Grandpa?" I said.

"Be patient," Grandpa said. He turned and looked at the map.

Me and Gracie did too.

We waited.

And waited.

Nothing happened.

"Hurry up and blink, you dumb old thing," said Gracie. Her voice shook.

"Sh-h-h," said Grandpa. He patted her back. "It'll be all right."

Then . . .

A red light blinked on the map.

Gracie laughed. "They're talking to us."

"Mr. Edison said we'll bring Mom and Dad home someday," I said. I pointed to the map. "So let's find out where we're going next."

Gracie nodded.

"I still don't like it," Grandpa said. He had his worried face on. "If only I could stop Crowe from chasing you."

"We'll be okay," Gracie said. "I'm not afraid. And George is smart. We both are."

I couldn't believe she said it. I pushed at my glasses. "Sure are," I said. "Thanks, Gracie."

"Don't get a big head over it," she said. She punched my shoulder.

The light blinked.

And blinked.

And blinked some more. Like it was saying, "What are you waiting for?"

Grandpa took my hand. And he took Gracie's.

He smiled down at us. "Okay then, kids. It's time," he said.

We stepped up to the map.

THE END . . . OR IS IT?

Thomas Edison and His Light Bulb

"Hi. This is Gracie."

"And this is George. We're going to tell you the true story of Thomas Edison and his light bulb. And Gracie's going to start. Right Gracie?"

"Right, George. Okay. Here goes. Thomas Edison was born in Milan, Ohio, on February 11, 1847. His father, Samuel Edison Jr., ran a shingle and grain business. His mother, Nancy Elliott Edison, taught school before she got married to Samuel. Thomas was the baby of the family. Everyone called him 'Al.'"

"Where did the name 'Al' come from, Gracie?"

"'Alva' is Thomas's middle name, George. 'Al' is short for 'Alva.'"

"Oh."

"Anyway. When Thomas turned seven, his family moved to Port Huron, Michigan. Right up next to Lake Huron. That's one of the Great Lakes."

"Everybody knows that, Gracie."

"Can I finish, please, George? Thomas was curious about the machines in the factories in Port Huron. He was curious about a lot of stuff. Except for school—he only went to school for a year or two for his whole life. Why? Because he daydreamed a lot in class. His teacher said Thomas had a fuzzy brain. That made Mrs. Edison mad. She told the teacher he was wrong. Then she took Thomas out of school. That's how his mom got to be his teacher."

"Don't forget to tell them that his mother was smart, Gracie. She gave him tons of books to read. That's why he loved reading so much."

"Right, George. Do you remember his favorite book?"

"Um . . . was it a book about math, Gracie? No, it was science. It had a long name, I think."

"A huge name, George. I wrote the name down

on a piece of paper. Just a second . . . the paper is in my pocket."

"Hurry up, Gracie. We won't have time to tell the rest of the story."

"Take a breath, George. Okay. Here it is. The book is called *A School Compendium of Natural and Experimental Philosophy*. Whew! That's one big fat title. Thomas loved that book because it talked about how machines work. And about electricity. And sound. And light. And about how magnets work. And about the stars and planets."

"Don't forget the telegraph, Gracie. The book also showed a drawing of the electric telegraph."

"I didn't forget, George. Stop interrupting me."

"Sorry, Gracie. Are you almost done?"

"One more part, George. The electric telegraph is how people sent messages in Thomas Edison's time. Like the telegraph that Mom and Dad send us messages on. Okay, George. Now it's your turn."

"Thanks, Gracie. Thomas didn't just read about science. He tried the experiments in his book. Like when he built his own electric telegraph set. Thomas stretched a wire from his house to his friend's house. Then they practiced sending Morse Code messages to each other. How cool is that, Gracie? We oughtta try it."

"Maybe later, George."

"Yeah, okay. Like I said, Thomas liked to experiment with stuff. When Thomas turned fifteen, he sold newspapers at railroad stations. He wanted to learn how to use the telegraph machine, though. This is where the story gets good, Gracie."

"I love this part, George."

"One day, Thomas saw a little boy climbing on the railroad tracks. A loud whistle blew. Thomas looked up. And there was a train. Coming right toward the little boy. So—"

"So Thomas grabbed the boy off the tracks in the nick of time. Right, George? George?"

"I'm not speaking to you, Gracie."

"Why?"

"You ruined my story."

"It's not ruined, George. Thomas was a hero. He saved the little boy."

"Graa-ciee . . ."

"Sorry. Go ahead."

"So, anyway the little boy's father was a telegraph operator. He said he would give Thomas lessons on the telegraph as a reward, which is how Thomas learned to work the telegraph. He got really good.

But just working the telegraph was boring to him. He wanted to make it better. He wanted to do his experiments. So he started a business fixing electrical machines. He worked hard. He saved his money. Then he got his own laboratory in Newark, New Jersey. He experimented with electrical machines there. And that's how he became a full-time inventor. Tell them about the light bulb, Gracie."

"Sure, George. Most people know about Thomas Edison because he invented the light bulb."

"He didn't invent the light bulb, Gracie. The light bulb was already invented. Thomas made it better. He made it stay lit up for hours and hours and hours and—"

"Uh, I thought I was telling the story, George? Would you stop talking? We only have two more pages left."

"Right, Gracie."

"This is a good story. Thomas built a new laboratory on a farm in Menlo Park, New Jersey. He called it the Invention Factory. He made seventy-five inventions in two years there. Including the phonograph, which is like an old-time record player—if you know what that is. The long-burning light bulb was his biggest invention, though. But it was a hard one to figure out. Here's why: Inside the bulb is a thing called a filament. It's what makes the bulb glow. Light bulbs in Thomas's time didn't burn very long. So he and his assistants worked hard to find a better filament. They burned more than 1,600 different kinds of things in their experiments. Like horsehair, coconut hair, bamboo, and spider webs. Thomas even burned his assistant's beard."

"No he did not, Gracie. That would burn his assistant's face off."

"He clipped the hair off his assistant's beard first, George. Gee."

"Oh. Okay, then. Go ahead, Gracie."

"Thanks a lot, George. Well, the beard didn't work anyway. Nothing burned long enough. One day Thomas rolled a piece of burned cotton thread called carbon between his fingers, and he got the idea to try the burned thread in the bulb. It worked! The carbon burned for thirteen hours. Thomas and his assistants kept working on the carbon until they made the bulb burn longer and longer. Then they invented a way to light up whole houses. And streets. And towns. And then the whole world. The End."

"Not The End, Gracie."

"Yes it is, George."

"Not yet. You forgot to say that Thomas Edison made more inventions than anyone in the world ever has. But he's famous because of the light bulb."

"You're such a show off, George. *You* forgot to say that he loved birds. He had *six* kids. *And* he couldn't hear well since he was a teenager. Bad hearing ran in his family."

"Oh, yeah, Gracie—what about the smart things he always said? Like 'Genius is one percent inspiration and ninety-nine percent perspiration.' That means if you work hard you can invent awesome stuff too. Like Edison's time machine."

"Thomas Edison didn't invent the time machine in real life, George."

"How do you know, Gracie?"

"Say goodbye, George."

"Goodbye, George."

"Very funny."

New Jersey State Facts

- **Statehood:** December 18, 1787, the third state to ratify the Constitution of the United States
- **Origin of the Name** *New Jersey***:** Named in 1664 by James, the Duke of York, for Jersey, a British Island in the English Channel
- **State Capital:** Trenton
- **State Flag:** The New Jersey State Flag was adopted in 1896. Its official color is buff, which is a yellowish-tan color. The colors of the state flag, buff and dark blue (Jersey blue), were the colors George Washington chose for the flag of New Jersey's army regiments during the Revolutionary War. The state seal is featured on the flag.
- **State Nickname:** "The Garden State"
- **State Song:** "I'm From New Jersey"
- **State Motto:** "Liberty and Prosperity"
- **State Flower:** Mountain Laurel
- **State Tree:** Purple Violet
- **State Bird:** Eastern Goldfinch
- **State Insect:** Honeybee
- **State Colors:** Jersey blue (dark blue) and Buff

New Jersey
State Curiosities

- New Jersey–born Aaron Burr, the vice president of the United States at the time, killed Alexander Hamilton in a duel in Weehawken, New Jersey, on July 11, 1804.

- The passenger airship Hindenburg was destroyed in a tragic mid-air fire on May 6, 1937, at Lakehurst, New Jersey. An airship looks like a giant, flying balloon and is also called a zeppelin.

- Many historians say that Hoboken, New Jersey, is the place where the first organized baseball game took place in 1846.

- College football became a sport when the Rutgers University and Princeton University football teams played each other on November 6, 1869, in New Brunswick, New Jersey.

- Grover Cleveland, 22nd and 24th president of the United States, was born in Caldwell, New Jersey, on March 18, 1837.

- Albert Einstein, world-famous physicist, lived in Princeton, New Jersey, after moving to the

United States before World War II. He died in Princeton in 1955.

- The first submarine was built in 1878 by John P. Holland, who was from the Passaic River Valley. The Passaic River at Patterson, New Jersey, was also the site of the first submarine ride by John P. Holland on May 22, 1878.

- The science of studying dinosaur fossils (called paleontology) began in 1858 when diggers discovered the complete skeleton of a dinosaur, the Hadrosaurus, in Haddonfield, New Jersey. The Hadrosaurus is the official New Jersey state dinosaur.

- The first robot to replace a human worker was used by General Motors in Ewing Township, New Jersey, in 1961.

- The first saltwater taffy was made at the Jersey shore in the 1870s.

- The first balloon flight in America was made by Jean-Pierre Blanchard. On January 9, 1793, he landed a balloon at Deptford, New Jersey, carrying a letter from George Washington.

- The first town to be lighted by electricity was Roselle, New Jersey in 1883.

Meet the Authors

Cheri Pray Earl writes the voice of George in the *Just In Time* series. She says that raising four sons makes her an expert at writing boys. She has an M.A. in Creative Writing from Brigham Young University and has taught college writing and literature for over twenty years; in her other life, she writes novels for young adults and adults. She has four sons and four daughters-in-law, one daughter and one son-in-law, five grandchildren (with more on the way), two dogs, and a cat. Cheri lives with her husband, Jeff, in Utah.

Carol Lynch Williams is the author of more than 25 books for kids and teen readers. She runs Writing and Illustrating for Young Readers, has an MFA in Writing for Children and Adolescents from Vermont College, and writes on an active blog with fellow writers Ann Dee Ellis and Kyra Leigh Williams (www.throwingupwords.wordpress.com). She teaches creative writing at Brigham Young University. Her books include *The Chosen One*, *Glimpse*, *Miles from Ordinary*, and *Waiting* with

Signed, *Sky Harper*, and *The Haven* forthcoming. She is proudest of her five daughters who are Carol's most perfect creative effort, ever. She and Cheri have been best friends for almost 20 years.

Meet the Illustrator

Manelle Oliphant graduated from BYU-Idaho with her illustration degree. She loves illustrating historical stories and fairytales. She lives with her husband in Salt Lake City, Utah. You can see her work and download free coloring pages on her website at www.manelleoliphant.com.

Where will the time machine land next? Get a sneak peak at:

just-in-time-books.com

You'll also find tons of fun ways to learn more about state history and explore the *Just in Time* books.